Jean-Henri Müntz, Anne C. P. Caylus

Encaustic

Count Caylus's method of painting in the manner of the ancients - to which is

added a sure and easy method for fixing of crayons

Jean-Henri Müntz, Anne C. P. Caylus

Encaustic
Count Caylus's method of painting in the manner of the ancients - to which is added a sure and easy method for fixing of crayons

ISBN/EAN: 9783337392376

Printed in Europe, USA, Canada, Australia, Japan

Cover: Foto ©Andreas Hilbeck / pixelio.de

More available books at **www.hansebooks.com**

ENCAUSTIC:

O R,

Count CAYLUS's

METHOD of PAINTING

In the MANNER of the ANCIENTS.

To which is added

A fure and eafy METHOD for Fixing of
CRAYONS.

By J. H. MÜNTZ.

LONDON: Printed for the AUTHOR; and
A. WEBLEY, at the BIBLE and CROWN near
CHANCERY LANE, HOLBORN, 1760.

TO THE

RIGHT HONOURABLE

Richard Lord Edgcumbe,

Controller of his MAJESTY's
Houſehold.

My LORD,

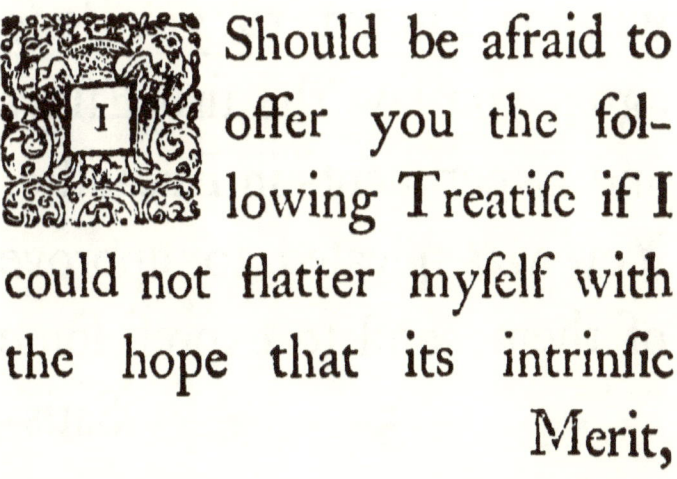 Should be afraid to
offer you the fol-
lowing Treatiſe if I
could not flatter myſelf with
the hope that its intrinſic
Merit,

Merit, and the Intention it was writ in, would in your noble and generous Mind counterballance the Defects and Improprieties of Language, of which, as almoſt unavoidable to a Foreigner, it muſt of courſe be guilty of.

The ſubject I preſent you with is known to you long ago; you ſaw the firſt Eſſays and Experiments in Encauſtic; You was pleaſed to approve of them, and to expreſs ſome

5   Satis-

Satisfaction at the least Picture executed in this manner. With what greater Advantage could I usher this new Invention into the World, than dedicating it to You; to make it known that the GREATEST PATRON of Arts, and the best Judge of the Merits of Painting approved of it?—Count CAYLUS invented it; under the Sanction of your Lordship's Name I offer it to the Public, and with a grateful

Sense

Senfe for all the Favours and Kindnefs You have at all Times fhewn towards me.

I am, my Lord,

your Lordfhip's

moft obedient

and moft obliged

humble Servant,

J. H. MÜNTZ.

ENCAUSTIC:

OR,

METHOD of PAINTING

In the Manner of the ANCIENTS.

A Relation of my proceedings, to reduce this singular invention into a regular system agreeable to reason, and practical in itself, would be tedious and superfluous : To enter upon the process without giving the reader some little account of the matter, would be improper. As something is required to introduce the reader, and as the books

B   I must

I muſt refer to are not in every body's poſſeſſion, I ſhall in *lieu of introduction*, inſert the whole as laid before the Royal Society,—which is as follows.

EXTRACT of a LETTER*
From the Abbé MAZEAS, F. R. S.

Concerning an ancient Method of Painting. Revived by Count CAYLUS.

COunt CAYLUS, a member of the Academy of Inſcriptions, had undertaken to explain an obſcure paſſage in PLINY the naturaliſt. This author (whom I have not now before me) ſays in ſome place of his works, that " the ancients painted with burnt wax."
and

* Philoſoph. Tranſact. vol. xlix. part 2.

* and we have it from tra-
dition, that pictures of this
kind were very durable.

B 2   This

* Though the Abbé does not quote the
paſſage, one may gueſs it muſt be the following
the count undertook to explain. *Pliny* lib. xxxv.
chap. 11.

" Ceris pingere ac picturam inurere quis pri-
mus excogitaverit non conſtat : quidam Ariſtidis
inventum putant, poſteà conſummatum à Prax-
itele. Sed aliquanto vetuſtiores Encauſticæ
Picturæ exſtitere, ut Polignoti & Nicanoris, &
Arceſilai Pariorum. Lyſippus quoque Æginæ
Picturæ ſuæ inſcripſit, ἐνεχαυσεν, quod profecto
non feciſſet niſi encauſtica inventa."

Which may be told in plain Engliſh thus, " Who
firſt invented to paint with (or in) wax, and
burn in (or fix) the picture with fire, is not
certainly known. Some think Ariſtides invented
it, and that Praxiteles brought it to perfection ;
but there were pictures by maſters, of a much
older date ; ſuch as of Polignote, Nicanor and
Arceſilaus, all artiſts of Paros.

Lyſippus writ upon his pictures he burnt in,
which he would not have done if the encauſtic
had not been invented then."

This was the paſſage, the count undertook to clear up, in trying all the different ways that are poſſible to paint in wax ; and after many experiments, he hit upon a very ſimple method, of which he made a ſecret, in order to excite the curioſity of the public.

The ſeveral artiſts who were deſirous of knowing by what means the count came to make this diſcovery, made ſeveral attempts themſelves ; but in a great number of trials, only two are worth mentioning.

The firſt was to melt wax and oil of turpentine together,
and

and uſe it for mixing the colours. But this method does not
at all explain PLINY's meaning;
becauſe wax is not burnt in
this way of managing it : and
beſides, this method has two
defects ; the oil of turpentine
dries too faſt, and does not al-
low the painter ſufficient time
to blend and unite his colours.

The ſecond method is very
ingenious, and ſeems to come
up to PLINY's notion very well;
it is as follows ; the wax is
melted with ſtrong lixivium of
ſalt of tartar, and with this the
colours are ground. When the
picture is finiſhed, it is gradually put to the fire, which in-

creaſes

creaſes the heat by degrees ;
the wax melts, ſwells, and is
bloated up upon the picture ;
then the picture is removed
gradually from the fire, and
the colours do not at all appear to have been diſordered ;
the colours then become unal-
terable by the action of the
fire, and even ſpirit of wine
has been burnt upon them
without doing them the leaſt
harm.

However, the following is
the Count de Caylus's me-
thod, which is much more
ſimple ; according to which
the head of Minerva was painted,

ed, which was fo much admired by all the connoiffeurs.

Firft. The cloth or wood defigned for the picture is waxed over, by only rubbing it fimply with a piece of beeswax.

Secondly. The colours are mixed up with common water; but as thefe colours will not adhere to the wax, the whole picture is to be firft rubbed over with Spanifh chalk, or whitening, and then the colours are ufed.

Thirdly. When the picture is dry, it is put near the fire,

B 4 whereby

whereby the wax melts, and abforbs all the colours.

It muft be allowed, that nothing can be more fimple than this method ; and it is thought, that this kind of painting is capable of with-ftanding the injuries of the weather, and laft longer than painting in oil; which I will not anfwer for.

The effect produced by thefe colours upon wax is very fin-gular ; nor can one have any notion of it without feeing it. The colours have not that na-tural varnifh or fhining, that they acquire with oil ; but you

are

are capable of feeing the picture in any light, or in whatfoever fituation you place it; in fhort there can be no falfe glare or light upon the picture for the fpectators: the colours are fe-cured, are firm, and will bear wafhing; and have a property, which I look upon as the moft important of any, which is, that they have fmoaked this picture in places fubject to foul vapours, and to fmoke in chim-nies; and then by being expo-fed to the dew, it became as clean as if it had been but juft painted."

Thefe are all the contents of the letter, laid before the Roy-al al Society by a member of that learned body, who accompanied it with a ſeries of very acute and learned obſervations, which, with an extenſive knowledge, ſhew an inclination to prove that the count's method could not be the encauſtic of the ancients, and that *encauſto pingendi* could be nothing elſe but enameling.——

It is neither my buſineſs nor intention to enter into diſcuſſions; it would be too difficult a taſk to prove that the count's invention comes up to PLINY's meaning; no certain evidence can be brought neither for nor againſt it. Any diſcovery that

tends

tends towards improvement of arts and ſciences is valuable; that the count's invention is of this kind, will appear to every unprejudiced mind.

Therefore it matters not if the ancients did ſo or not.

But, to give my opinion on-ly——— the numberleſs experiments I made to bring the new encauſtic into a regular ſyſtem —the repeated trials to explain PLINY's meaning any other way that would anſwer the general ends of painting, &c. induce me to believe that *encauſto pin-gendi* of the ancients could not be enameling, but muſt have
been

been ſome manner of painting very near of kin to that which is the ſubject of this treatiſe. Beſides the clear and expreſſive words of our ancient author— *Ceris pingere ac pičturam inurere*—and where he ſpeaks of their ſhip painting—*reſolutis igni ceris penicilio utendi*—carry a ſilent proof with them, that the Latin verb *urere* ought not to be underſtood in ſo fierce a degree as enameling requires. *

In both the above cited paſages *cera* is in the plural number ;

* Pliny is an evidence for this my opinion; for after having ſaid, lib. xxxv. ch. 4. *Nicias ſcripſit ſe inuſſiſſe*, he ſays, *tali enim uſus eſt verbo*. Which words ſeem clearly to indite that Pliny thought it equivocal, or contrary to its proper ſignification.

ber ; and for this very reafon I
believe it can mean nothing elfe
but bees-wax fimple, or com-
pounded with other ingredients
capable to fympathife there-
with.

It would be ridiculous to
fuppofe the Latin tongue fo
defective in PLINY's time,
as not to afford two diftinct
names for two things fo oppo-
fite as enameling and fhip
painting are.

I cannot conceive what good
enamel would or could do to
their fhips, without undergo-
ing the operation of the fire
after being painted. Nor can I
form

form any idea of a Roman ena-
meled firſt-rate man of war.

The moſt probable reaſon,
for PLINY's not giving a better
account of particulars may be,
that he knowing nothing at all
of the matter, uſed the term of
art then in vogue ; or was im-
poſed upon by artiſts who did
not chuſe to part with the ſecret of their art.

Inſtances of this kind we
have every day.——— Arts and
trades abound with jargon and
myſtical names, which, if taken
or explained literally, would
often prove but little analogous
to their ſubject. Writers that
pay

pay no regard to that, and
without farther ſcrutiny ſpeak
and relate what they are told,
muſt of courſe be unintelligible.
Hence it comes that moſt of
our dictionaries on arts and ſciences, and the greateſt num-
ber of books on painting, are
ſo perplexing; and in many
a point rival PLINY in obſcu-
rity.

To write upon a ſubject and
unfold its myſtery, one ought
to be practically acquainted
with it; a ſuperficial drawing
is not enough; to teach others
how to go to work, the ſection
is wanted.

If

If all books upon arts and ſciences, manufactures and me- chanics, had been or could be written by the reſpective pro- feſſors thereof, things would appear in another light; we ſhould, perhaps, not have the fineſt language in thoſe per- formances; but we do not want that, plain truth and common ſenſe is all that is required; if a guide leads us the right way, we need not mind his dreſs.

I ſhall make no apology for this performance of mine: if the contents do not ſpeak for themſelves, my abilities as a writer would but weakly ſup- port them, only as new inven- tions

tions are frequently condemn-
ed for no other reaſon but becauſe they are new ; it becomes
me to acquaint the public, that
I ſhould never have gone ſo
far as to publiſh this ſyſtem, if
I had not been convinced of
its merit by experience and
practice ; I made many and
various experiments (as will be
mentioned in the ſequel) to aſ-
certain its ſtability ; and having painted ſeveral pictures of
different ſizes, I can anſwer for
its practicability. In ſhort, it
is a manner of painting ſuſcep-
tible of all the boldneſs, freedom and delicacy of any other
whatſoever ; you may leave off
and cheriſh your work at plea-

C ſure,

ſure, you cannot fatigue your colours, you are not ſubject to that inconvenience attending oil painting, viz. of ſetting one's picture by to dry, &c.

You will have all the effects and ſweetneſs of painting in oil, and the colours will not be liable to fade and change; no damp can affect it, no corroſive will hurt it; nor can the colours crack and fall in ſhivers from off the canvas.

Let no-body think me too poſitive, or intoxicated with my own notions, before they have gone through the whole treatiſe, and made a few experiments.

ments. I advance facts, and not conjectures only.

It is not my intention to quarrel or depreciate oil painting, nor will I attempt to deny its true merit; therefore hope it will not be confidered as a crime to propofe a method that will equal its perfections, and furpafs it for duration and ftability of colours. I tell artifts what I know, they may do what they judge proper. Though I beftow encomiums upon my fubject it is not with a defign to impofe; I am not felf-conceited, or foolifh enough to think or believe that Rynolds or Ranfey, Scott or

Lam-

Lambert, &c. &c. will take up at once and prefer my new' ſyſtem to that they practiſed for many years with ſucceſs and applauſe—they, and every body elſe, may try ; a trifling expence, and a few idle hours will afford experiments by which they will know if what I advance will really be an advantage to their works and themſelves. And how far it will anſwer, either whole or in part, the general ends of painting, one ſingle ſketch will be enough to judge by ; in arts, one experience is worth a thouſand conjectures.

In

In the profecution of my fyftem, oil colours came always in for a part of the experiment, in oppofition to thofe fixed with wax, in order to judge better and with more precifion of their variation. By this it happened that I often painted oil colours over a waxed ground ; which colours always appeared brighter and cleaner than the very fame painted over an oil cloth; at leaft I fancied that dead colouring in water colours and finifhing in oil, was an experiment worth trying. For this purpofe (as portrait painting is not my province) I pitched upon a head of Sir Godfrey Kneller, a gentleman and friend had

C 3   fent

fent me to copy fmall in oil;
accordingly I dead coloured it
in water colours and fixed them
with wax, and afterwards finifhed it in oil colours, not
only to my fatisfaction and fur-
prize, but every body's elfe that
faw it; the brightnefs and tranf-
parency of its colours is not to
be conceived. I copied the fame
head again in oil colours only,
and with all imaginable care
and attention, but the colouring of the latter looked dull in
oppofition to the other *; to
give reafons for this incident
is

---

* Both pictures were difpofed of as foon as
finifhed to a Dutch gentleman, who fent them
to Holland as a pattern, and were might ly approved of.

is more than I can do ; I ſhall give a few conjectures, and con-jectures only, upon it, under the article of experiments.

If I ſhould not gain the ap-probation and good will of the oil painting faculty, for a few hints : I am ſure thoſe artiſts who profeſs painting in cray-ons will be beholden to me for what I ſhall communicate to them—a method to fix cray-ons or paſtelle.

Every body knows the beau-ties and pleaſing effects of thoſe paintings and their periſhable qualities ſo well, that to en-large upon is needleſs to be-

ſtow

ſtow great encomiums upon my
ſecret, which is ſo cloſely connected with encauſtic for the
pencil, and whoſe merit has already been mentioned, would
be ſuperfluous; the proceſs and
experiments I am now going
to unfold will be of more weight
than all my reaſonings previous
thereto.

To make the whole familiar
and eaſy to all capacities, I
thought it convenient to lay
down the whole penciling ſyſtem under five different articles
or periods, according as they
ſucceed each other in the execution ; and to keep the thread
of the proceeding uninterrupt-
ed,

ed, I ſhall make a few obſervations upon every article in
particular, and there give and
explain the different methods
that may be practiſed for the
ſame end, together with my
reaſon, and why I deviated in
ſome parts from Count C A Y-
L U S's ſyſtem.

The operations for painting
with crayons will be treated and
explained ſeparately, and upon the ſame plan. Laſtly, the
experiments will come in to illuſtrate both, and verify what
I advance.

A R T. I.

Preparation of the cloth for painting in Encauſtic.

TAKE any ſort of clean linnen cloth whoſe texture is pretty cloſe, ſoft and even, ſtretch it upon a ſtraining frame, as you would do an oil cloth, lay it upon a ſmoth table, the ſide your are to paint on downwards, then with a piece of common bees or virgin wax rub it over and over, till you perceive a good quantity of the wax adhere to the cloth, in equal proportion over the whole. *

Your

* Any ſort of old cloth, if whole, is as good as new; I prefer the former to the latter ſor its
ſoft-

Your cloth thus waxed is ready to paint upon if it be fine; if it is coarfe, turn it, and with a pumice ftone gently rub over the fide which is to receive the colours, to take off all the knots and unevennefs that might obftruct the free flowing of your pencil.

If you want to paint a picture of any determined fize, provide a ftraining frame, whofe inner circumference is equal to the height and width required; that is to fay, you muft have

softnefs. To afcertain a juft proportion of wax to every fort of cloth is unneceffary, if you fhould either put too much or not enough, you may eafily remedy it. See ART. iv. One fingle trial will clear up the incertitude.

have two fra^{mes}, the one to
work and fi nifh your picture
upon, the other whereon the
picture is to go and remain
when finifhed. The firft muft
be of fuch height and width,
as to contain between its inner
edges cloth enough to cover
the fecond. No part of the
cloth you paint over ought to
touch the wood of the frame,
if it did the wood would imbibe part of the wax, when
the picture is brought near the
fire, and leave thofe parts im-
perfect.

A R T. II.

Of the colours and their pre-paration.

ALL colours uſed in oil painting are fit for this manner, and no others. There are a few that ought to be omitted ; for reaſon ſee the liſt of colours.

Grind all your colours very fine with ſimple wa-ter, allot to every particular colour a diſtinct veſſel, ſuch as galipots, pans, &c. From your colours ſo ground, compoſe all the different principal tints, as the

the nature of your intended work ſhall require.

But, as moſt of the colours acquire a deeper hue when moiſtened, and ſome deeper ſtill when fixed with wax, it will be neceſſary, to prevent perplexity in the execution, to have a guide for retouching, either when the picture is fi-niſhed and dry, before the operation of the fire, or after it is fixed; for this purpoſe you may, before you go to work, uſe the following expedient.

Take two ſlips of cloth a-bout a foot long, and three or four

four inches wide, wax them as before mentioned, then up-on the one flip paint of every one of your entire colours * a-bout an inch high over the whole width of the cloth, and with yonr tints already com-pofed do the fame upon the other piece of cloth, according to their order and degradation; † mark every tint with a num-ber, fuch as 1, 2, 3, &c. write down upon a paper every num-ber, and what it is compofed of. This done and your co-lours fo applied dry, cut your cloth acrofs all the tints from

top.

* Entire colours are the white, red, yellow blue, &c.

† See the nature of this better explained in the copper-plate at the end of obfervations of Art. 2.

top to bottom in two equal
parts; bring one half of each
near the fire, and by melting
the wax fix them, the other
two halves you keep as they
are unfixed.

By rejoining and comparing
them together, you may judge
what ftrength every tint will
acquire, and by their recipro-
cal references you will be ena-
bled to alter or imitate, deepen
or heighten with certainty, any
tint, either before or after the
colours are fixed.

In painting be not fparing;
the greater body of colours you
employ, the better and brighter
your

your work will appear ; you
may give greater freedom to
your pencil, blend and fweet-
en your colours better than in
any other way of painting.

A R T. III.

*How to paint over or alter any
part before the picture has
been near the fire.*

IF the parts of the picture
you want to retouch are large
and the colouring dry, take a
large foft hair pencil, and with
water gently moiften thofe places, or the whole picture if you
pleafe, and repaint till your
eye is fatisfied. You might

D   paint

paint over, or alter any part without moiſtening, but on a firſt trial you would not ſo well ſee what you are about. While the picture is wet it appears very near what it will be when fixed; when it is dry it looks like a weak dead colouring in oil. You will ſee enough to judge of the general effect, but none of the tenderer half tints will appear diſcernable enough to judge of them with preciſion. In large pictures where the cloth will be required ſtronger, a picture is kept wet with great eaſe and ſecurity, by moiſtening it on the back with a large bruſh as often as there is occaſion, for the

water

water will ſoon ſoak through the texture and take hold of the colours; there is no danger of diſturbing them on the other ſide with the action of the bruſh, by reaſon of the ſubſtance of the cloth.

A R T. IV.

To fix the colours by melting the wax.

WHEN your picture is fi-niſhed and dry, have a good clear fire of ſea-coals, *

D 2　　approach

---

* I prefer a fire of ſea-coals becauſe it is much more uniform, and does not emit ſo many ſparks as wood or charcoals, which might in-jure the picture, though any fire with proper care will anſwer the end propoſed; a German ſtove is ſtill better than any fire whatſoever.

approach your picture with the painted fide towards it, at about two feet diftance, let it grow warm by gentle degrees, always approaching nearer, till within a foot diftance from the grate, but never clofer, holding your picture perpendicularly or a little inclined as you fhall find neceffary. If the picture is large do one half firft, then the other; there is not the leaft difficulty for any fize.

When you perceive by the hue and fhining of the painted furface that all is perfectly abforbed; then remove it gradually from the fire as you advanced

vanced it, and your picture
will be done.

If you ſee any place defective for want of a ſufficient
quantity of wax, * put a little
finely ſcraped wax on the back
of that place, then bring only
a red hot poker, or ſome ſuch
thing towards it, the wax will
immediately ſettle in its place.
If there are many parts ſo defective, put ſcrapings of wax
there, and bring the whole picture before the fire as above
mentioned. There is no danger in bringing the picture to

D 3   the

* You will eaſily know thoſe places that
ſhall want wax ; they will appear like ſo many
ſpots of a lighter hue.

the fire as often as required,
provided you never give it too
great a degree of heat; if you
do, the wax will raife in bubbles upon the furface, and your
picture will look rough and
uneven,

Advance your picture never
too hafty, nor retire it too quick-
ly; if you do the former, the
fudden action of the fire might
difturb fome of the colours; if
the latter, the wax will not retire enough within the texture
of the cloth, confequently lye
too much above the colours and
look glaring. If you perceive
any fuch glaring fpots or places upon your picture, or (in
other

other words) parts that appear varnifhed like, and that appearance fhould proceed from too great a quantity of wax, paint thofe places over on the back with whitening, or any one of your other colours, and when dry bring the picture near the fire, as above mentioned, and thofe colours or whitening will imbibe the overplus of the wax. Repeat that if required.

A R T. V.

How to retouch or paint over any part after the colours are fixed.

PUT upon your pallet such of your tints as will be fit for the place or parts you want to alter or paint over, temper and employ them with a little spirit of wine ; * repaint, and bring the picture to the fire as often as required, and those retouched parts will become fixed

---

* Any other spirit such as that commonly burnt in lamps, common gin, rum, or genuine brandy, will do just as well ; spirit or oil of turpentine is very proper too ; but as it smells so very strong, ladies and gentlemen that paint for their amusement only would not like it.

fixed like any other part of the picture.

Obſervations on article the firſt.

AS linen cloth is the material moſt commonly and preferably uſed, as the fitteſt and moſt convenient to paint upon, I choſe to give under Article the firſt, directions for that purpoſe only ; for though the wax and colours may be applied to cloth and other materials in ſeveral different manners, I, not to bewilder the beginners in multiplicities on a firſt ſetting out, gave and recommend that, which beſides

its

its being the likelieſt to be moſt practiſed, is the beſt for solidity, and will prove to every practitioner the eaſieſt, moſt agreeable, expeditious and convenient for execution.

But not to deprive the artiſts and curious of the ſeveral means and methods that may be practiſed for and towards the ſame end, I ſhall here give ſome of the principal ones, as well for painting upon canvas as upon wood, plaiſter, &c. but firſt of all I ſhall conſider and treat Count Caylus's ſyſtem a little more at large, and ſhew why I have deviated from it in this particular, and leave
the

the artiſt at liberty to adopt and practiſe which ſuits him beſt.

The Count's method for preparing the cloth conſiſts, in ſtretching it upon a frame, and holding it horizontally over, or perpendicularly before a fire (at a diſtance convenient and proportionable to the degree of heat it caſts) and rubbing it with a piece of wax ; which, melting gradually as it is rubbed on, diffuſes itſelf, penetrates the body, and fills the interſtices of the texture of the cloth, which when cool, is fit to paint upon; but, as water colours will not adhere regularly flowing and

con-

connectedly to the wax, He, to
remedy this inconveniency,
makes uſe of an intermediate
body, viz. chalk or whitening,
with which he rubs over that
ſurface of the waxed canvas
he intends to paint upon, and
then the colours will eaſily flow
over and adhere to it.

Now, though this way of
proceeding is very ſimple and
ſuccefsfully practicable for ſmall
ſubjects;—for inſtance,—ſuch
as the head of Diana, mentioned in the Abbè's letter, or
any other that may be finiſhed
in a couple of hours, and while
the colours upon the canvas
retain moiſture; yet, to exe-
cute

cute pictures of a larger fize
and compofition, which will
require many a day's labour and
application, and whereof no
part can be finifhed pofitively
at the firft onfet, this manner
of managing it will not anfwer
fo well, as that given under
Art. the firft, for the following
reafons.

Firft. In painting upon the
wax by virtue of the whitening,
you will not have that conveniency of retouching or alter-
ing of any part, and before the
colours are fixed, fo well, as
painting upon the raw and bare
canvas will afford you; becaufe the texture and fibres of
the

the cloth being thoroughly in-
vaded by the wax, there re-
mains nothing for water colours to fix or adhere to, capable to retain them ; thoſe colours once dry, the ſlighteſt
touch of a moiſt pencil will, as
it were, attract them, and frequently make and leave a bare
ſpot; ſo that in attempting to
retouch, inſtead of adding freſh
colours, you will fetch off the
old ones; for though the rough
edged particles of the chalk facilitate to the firſt colours an
adheſion upon the ſmooth body wax yet, water the vehi-
cle of the colours, being the
menſtruum of chalk, by diſ-
compoſing it deſtroys part of its
power

power and virtue, and renders
it incapable to perform the firft
fervice a fecond time.

Secondly. Upon canvas fully
imbibed with wax, you can
neither ufe fo great a body of
colours, nor employ them with
fuch freedom, boldncfs, or delicacy as you may upon cloth,
whofe texture is not pre-occupied
with wax—the reafon is obvi-
ous—the one has its pores and
interftices filled up with wax ;
the other's you muft fill up with
colours. Cloth, a firm fpungy
body or fubftance, in fucking
in the water attracts the colours
along with it into its pores,
and thereby facilitates the firm
and

and delicate ſtrokes; and the colours mixing and adhering to its numberleſs fibres, will not come off on retouching, before the picture is fixed; you may cheriſh or leave your work at pleaſure without detriment or inconveniency ariſing from that. Advantages that cloth pre-occupied with wax is incapable of.

Thirdly and laſtly. By painting on canvas prepared according to the directions of Art. the firſt, your works will be more ſolid and laſting, becauſe the colours will not ſimply lay upon the ſurface of the wax, but cloth, wax and colours will make

make but one individual body.
—Thus much on my deviation
from Count CAYLUS's ſyſtem,
in regard to the preparation of
the cloth.

For painting upon walls or
plaiſter where the wax cannot
be applied on the back, the
Count's ſyſtem muſt be practiſed ; it will ſucceed well ; the
rough and gritty grain of the
plaiſter will take and retain a
ſufficient quantity of colours to
inſure ſolidity ; the only difference between painting upon
cloth and plaiſter conſiſts in
this ; painting upon canvas you
can finiſh your picture intirely

E   before

before you fix it; in painting
upon plaiſter, you muſt proceed as you do in painting with
oil colours, viz. firſt, dead colour your ſubject and fix it,
and then paint it over again
and finiſh it, either by virtue
of the chalk, or by tempering
and employing the colours with
ſome ſpirit, or oil of turpentine.
You may too paint and retouch
with crayons.

Upon wood, ſtone, and me-
tals,—you muſt proceed as you
do upon plaiſter; but as there
is no grain you muſt procure
an artificial one, after your
board is waxed, by laying on a
ground

ground of any colour mixed with half chalk and fix it *; upon this you may paint with water colours or crayons, as fweetly as upon canvas.

To paint upon paper;—you muft have a fmooth board, or copper plate of a convenient fize, and well waxed; upon this you faften your paper by the corners and paint upon; the colours dry, prefent it to the fire, and the wax underneath the paper melting, will foak and penetrate through and

E 2   fix

* The fame might be practiced upon cloth, it would do better than only rubbing it with the chalk; but for painting with the pencil the bare cloth is ftill better.

fix the colours; this method may be fuccefsfully practifed with cloth.

There are two more methods remaining to be practifed on cloth and paper; but as they make part of the fyftem for painting with crayons, and will be defcribed under that head, I omit to mention them here.

*Obſervations on Article the ſe-
cond.*

IN grinding the colours upon
the ſtone, and managing
them upon the pallette, care
ſhould be taken not to uſe an
iron knife, the ſteel or iron that
grinds off, in mixing with the
colours ſpoils their brightneſs
and vivacity; flake-white and
white-lead, yellow-oker, lacque
and light-red, ſuffer greatly by
it, it gives them a dull and
dirty caſt; Naples-yellow ſuf-
fers moſt of all from it; its vivacity is entirely deſtroyed by
the iron's touching it. Horn,
ivory, or tortoiſe ſhell knives, or

E 3 wooden

wooden ſpatula's are fitter for
all manner of painting; they
will affect no colours; iron
knives have deſtroyed many a
tender complexion in oil colours ; for, the oil once dry,
the iron ground off from the
knife and mixed in the colours
will be converted into ruſt by
the moiſture of the air.——Tho'
this little hint is foreign to our
preſent ſubject, it will perhaps
not be unacceptable to my bre-
thren.——It is an eſſential point
in an architect to be acquainted with the qualities and pro-
perties of the materials he builds
with, if his plan and ſtile, diſ-
poſitions, proportions, &c. be
ever

ever ſo good, noble, grand and graceful, yet if his fabric falls down as ſoon as built, we are but little beholden to his ſkill. —Vandyke, I believe, never uſed an iron knife, if he had he would not have painted a ſpatula of horn in one of his pictures, wherein all the utenſils of a painter accompany his own figure.—

The expedient recommended under Art. the ſecond, for eſtabliſhing a ſtandard for all the differing principal tints that may be required for any ſubject, will be of uſe to them who are not much acquainted with painting in water colours;

E 4   and

and to ladies and gentlemen, who painting only now and then for their amuſement, cannot have ſo thorough a knowledge of the value of each colour, and might therefore be at a loſs how to retouch, after the colours are fixed.

To make the directions given for that purpoſe more intelligible, and to point out the uſe of ſuch a ſtandard—let us ſuppoſe—the annexed copper plate figure A. B. C. D. to be a piece of cloth, about a foot long and three or four inches wide, waxed on the back, as directed under Art. the firſt, and the diviſions a. b. c. d. e. f. g. h. &c. be the tints painted, accord-

according to their order and degradation, acrofs the whole width of the cloth A. B. thefe tints dry, cut the piece of cloth acrofs all the tints from top E. to bottom F. in two equal parts, bring the one half A C near the fire, and by melting the wax fix it, the other half B D you keep as it is unfixed.

Now, the half A C being fixed, will fhew you at one glance what ftrength every tint will acquire; and if you moiften again the other half B D, or paint the fame tints upon a frefh piece of cloth, you will fee which are the colours that grow deeper ftill, fixed with

wax

wax than they appear when
only moiſtened with water, and
the references 1 2 3 4 5 &c.
telling you what each tint is
compoſed of, you will be ena-
bled to amend any one that
might be amiſs. Farther, when
your picture will be fixed and
it ſhould want retouching, and
you ſhould be at a loſs for hit-
ting of the tint or hue required for that purpoſe,——bring
only the fixed half A C upon
the picture and compare them,
and you will eaſily find what
you want ; again, if you want
to renew any tint that is ſpent,
find that tint upon the picture,
with the fixed half A C, when
found compare it to, and
moiſten

A	*E*	B
I	*a*	1
2	*b*	2
3	*c*	3
4	*d*	4
5	*e*	5
6	*f*	6
7	*g*	7
8	*h*	8
9	*i*	9
10	*k*	10
C	*F*	D

moiften its fellow upon the unfixed half B D, and that will
give you again the original hue,
and the references 1 2 3 4 &c.
will tell you what that tint is
principally compofed of.

Tho' profeffed artifts (whofe
long experience enables them
to judge of the value of each
colour) will not have abfolute
occafion for the comparative
ufe of fuch a ftandard, yet they
will not do amifs to make an
effay of their tints before they
employ them.

Obfer-

Obſervations on Article the third.

THE being able to work and retouch at pleaſure, and at any time, without fatiguing the colours, or any other detriment ariſing from it, is an advantage peculiar to encauſtic only; for, the new colours will unite with the old ones without making ſpots, as is the caſe in common ſize-painting; nor will there be that inconveniency of rubbing the places to be retouched over with oil, as is the caſe with oil pictures; the only ſeeming difficulty to a beginner, will

conſiſt

confist in the colours growing
paler and weaker in drying,
but as a picture is easily kept
wet, by moistening it now and
then as above directed, the
difficulty vanishes. Pictures of
any size may easily be kept
wet for several days, by apply-
ing a double wet cloth on the
back ; but a little practice will
render that precaution unne-
cessary.

Every body in the least acquainted with colours, knows
that water colours, tempered
or employed either with gum
or size, grow paler and lighter
in drying, and that they acquire their true tone only when
dry ;

dry;—in encauſtic they grow paler and lighter too in drying, but they recede from and loſe their true tone.—Encauſtic is the reverſe of ſize-painting as to effect, while you are at work and the colours wet;— of the latter you cannot judge poſitively until the colours are dry; of the former you can only judge while the colours are wet, or which is the ſame, when fixed with the wax.

Obſervations on Article the fourth.

THE moſt eſſential point in encauſtic—the fixing of the colours—is the ſimpleſt and eaſieſt for paintings of any ſize, moveable or immoveable. A ſurface of forty feet may be fixed as conveniently as a picture of twelve inches; for if the painting be too large to be brought near the fire, or immoveable on a wall, bring that agent to the painting;———a ſquare copper or iron cheſt, or box, ſuch as commonly uſed for warming or airing of beds, with a red hot iron or lighted char-

charcoal in it, will do the bu-
finefs admirably well, by pafs-
ing it in a direction parallel to
and before the painted furface,
at a diftance proportionable to
the degree of heat it cafts,—a
brafier ambulant, with a cover
to prevent the afhes from fly-
ing about, with charcoal well
lighted, will anfwer the end
too, by inclining the picture
over it,—an inftrument of iron
like a baker's fhovel, with a
long handle and made red hot,
will perform the fame fervice,
if waved in a parallel direction
before the painted furface; and
by heating it again, when grown
cool, with fuch an inftrument
one may fix paintings of the
largeft

largeſt ſize; it matters not if the whole be fixed at once, or in parts at different times.

The direcions for rectifying of any defects ariſing from too ſmall a quantity of wax, are ſo clear, ſimple and ſufficient, that they want but little explanation or addition; only, you may inſtead of wax ſimple uſe wax diſſolved in ſuch a quantity of oil of turpentine, as to make it when cool, fluent enough to be employed with a bruſh on the back of the picture, which, when brought to the fire, the wax will ſettle with the colours, and the turpentine will fly off.

F   My

My faying under the above article that the fudden action of the fire might difturb fome of the colours, muft not be underftood in regard to the wax, but in regard to the nature of the colours, which, if the picture be brought too near the fire at once, will be fcorched before the wax can melt and penetrate the texture to fcreen and fecure them.

Obfer-

*Obſervations on Art. the fifth
and laſt.*

THE facility and conve-
niency for retouching a
picture after the colours are
fixed, without the new colours differing from the hue
of the old ones, is an advantage no other manner of painting is poſſeſſed of.

In oil-painting you cannot
do it ſo well except you paint
over large parts, becauſe the
colours in drying acquire a
yellower hue, than they have
while freſh ; there will always

be a difference between the very ſame tints; beſides, oil pictures are frequently greaſy-like and refuſe the new colours, ſo that you are obliged to rub thoſe parts with oil, to make the new colours adhere to and flow over the old ones, which rubbing with oil very often makes a dull and yellow ſpot when the colours are dry; in ſize-painting it is worſe, re-touchings there in general appear hard, and in large maſſes of a uniform colour,—ſuch as ſky's— produce ſpots.——Encauſtic is free from all that; you may glaze with a body of colours as thin and as tranſ-

parent.

parent as you pleafe, without your colours changing of tone. By retouching with crayons upon the fixed colours, the fweeteft effects may be produced in landfcapes and figures ; nay, for retouching only here and there, I fhould prefer crayons. For inftance—to finifh a head, —and give the decifive ftrokes about the eye, mouth, hair, and fharp folds of linen, &c. in landfcapes—for the extremities of trees, &c. the fmart touch of a crayon will be preferable to the pencil.

When your picture is intirely finifhed, and you fhould want

to give the canvas more solidity, you may paint it over on the back with any colour or tint, and bring it again and for the laſt time to the fire, to fix that colour ; if you apprehend there is not wax enough, apply a little diſſolved in ſpirit of turpentine, as mentioned in the foregoing obſervations on Art. iv. this fixed take your picture off from the frame, and ſtretch it upon that whereon it is to remain.

Having now done with the proceſs for painting in encauſtic with the pencil, which notwithſtanding its ſimplicity might

appear

appear to ſome beginners in-
tricate, becauſe I pointed out
all the difficulties that poſſibly
may occur in the execution,——
to comfort and encourage thoſe
that might think the taſk hard,
I ſhall recapitulate, and reduce the whole within this
compaſs.—— *Stretch a piece of
cloth upon a frame, rub the
back of that cloth with wax,
paint your ſubjeƈt on the other
ſide, with colours prepared and
tempered with water, and when
dry bring the piƈture near the
fire, and by melting the wax
fix the colours.*

N. B. I might have ſaid
much more, and dwelt longer
F 4 on

on ſeveral particulars ; but as the only aim of this treatiſe is to communicate the diſcovery to artiſts, and others already acquainted with the management of colours, and not to form pupils from beginning, I omitted ſaying any thing of compoſing the tints and diſpoſing the colours on the pallette, &c. Every artiſt may go on in his accuſtomed method ; the uſe of all the colours is in encauſtic as in oil, as may be ſeen by the following liſt.

The direction for painting with crayons will illuſtrate ſome paſſages of the foregoing proceſs, and what other advantages encauſtic

encauſtic painting will have over oil and ſize painting will be ſhewn by concluſions drawn from the experiments.

The end of the firſt part.

LIST

LIST of the COLOURS

To be USED for

Painting in Encauſtic;

AS ALSO FOR THE

COMPOSING of the CRAYONS.

WHITE.

Flake-white, and white-lead, or ceruſs.

FOR painting in encauſtic, I mix always both together half and half; flake white a-lone is ſubject to raiſe too much little bubbles in employing it

with

with water, which the admix-
ture of the other prevents; befides, both together make a
better and more folid body;
tho' flake white is the whiteft
of the two, to ufe either alone
I fhould prefer the fecond. The
Venetian or Dalmatian white
lead is by far the beft for all
manner of painting; being prepared with a purer and fubtler
acid it is whiter and purer than
any other whatfoever, and preferable to flake white; next to
it is the German or Dutch;
French or Englifh cerufs are in
general but indifferent, in experiments I frequently found
the latter to have one third of
marle or chalk in its compofition;

tion ; which is the cauſe of its growing ſo ſoon yellow, dull and dirty in oil.

In compoſing of the crayons it will be well to obſerve the above mentioned proportion of half and half, as by the doing ſo, much pipe clay will not be required to bind them.

YELLOWS.

Naples-yellow,
Light-oker,
Brown-oker,
Yellow-orpiment, or,
King's-yellow,
Red-orpiment,
are all perfectly good and ne-ceſſary for our purpoſe.

Naples-

Naples-yellow is the only colour that ought to be ufed in compofing the tenderer flefh tints of women; it proves a very tender, bright and beautiful lafting colour for all manner of painting, if properly prepared and managed, if not, a dirty, weak and treacherous one, and particularly in oil. It is a mineral compound of lead, antimony, fulphur, and fome arfenic, which latter is the caufe of its changing, and hurting other colours, and particularly the white, fo much complained of by the painters.

Though this yellow fixed with wax will not change; yet

it

it will not be amiſs to inſert a method to clean, and purify it, ſo as to render it beautiful and laſting for oil and other uſes. To clean it do as follows.

Take crude Naples-yellow, (the heavieſt for bulk is the beſt) and break it into ſmall pieces with the mallet upon the grinding ſtone, put it in a clean earthen veſſel, and pour over it a quantity of new milk, ſufficient to cover it three or four inches over, ſtirring it well for ſome time with a wooden ſpatula or ſtick; then let all together ſtand undiſturbed for five or ſix days, and the milk will become thick and ſour, and

maſter

master by its acidity the nox-
ious saline principles of the colour; having stood the abovementioned time, take off the
creamy part from the top of
the milk, and pour warm water upon it, and let the vessel
overflow till you perceive the
water to come off as clear as
when poured on, and the colour will be purified and fit
for use.

Light-oker, a precipitated,
feruginous earth, answers in encaustic all the purposes it does
in oil.

Brown-oker, a precipitated
feruginous earth too, only it
par-

partakes a little of a vitrioline principle, which the light oker does not. In encauſtic this colour anſwers all the purpoſes it does in oil.

Yellow orpiment, or king's yellow. The principal conſtituent particles of this colour are, ſulphur and arſenic, which latter prevails and makes great havock among the other colours when uſed in oil; it cannot play the ſame tricks fixed with wax; wax being a cloſer and unvariable body, confines its arſenical principle. Oil once dry ceaſes to be oil, and can confine them no longer.

Red-

Red-orpiment, fo called to diftinguifh it from the other, is properly not red, but of a rich orange colour, and is a compound of arfenic and ful-phur too; but here fulphur prevails, which is the reafon of its ftanding its ground better and doing lefs harm in oil than the other.

In encauftic it is of univer-fal ufe, throughout a whole picture to give warmth to lights and fhades; in landfcapes it may be ufed from the horizon down to the fore ground, to good purpofe; for fhades in flefh it is admirable, it gives a clear, foft and tranfparent ftrength;

in the verdure of landfcapes it anfwers all the ends for brown pink, when mixed with a little bone black.

This colour is very confpicuous in all the warmer landfcapes of Claude Lorraine; Mr. Vernet a famous French painter ufes it very much.

P I N K S.

Light-pink, and brown-pink.

Thefe two colours ought rather not be ufed, as they both proceed from the fame vegetable principle, viz. the juice or extract got by decoction from French berries by the help

help of acid falts ; confequently incapable to fympathife with or admit wax into their pores * ; the wax can take hold of them only fuperficially, which makes them appear dry and gritty up- on the picture, and will eafily come off by rubbing them with one's finger. Thofe artifts who cannot do without them, will do well to grind them, the light pink with a little light oker, and brown pink with a

G 2   little

---

* I am aware that every body will not en- ter into this doctrine at firft, and fome may think it very odd that a colour which is ufed in oil, fhould not fympathife with wax; the queftion is eafily folved, the grinding ftones unite oil and pinks, and bring them together by force, but experience fhews it is but for a little while ; the oil once dry, pinks foon fly off and fade away.

little brown oker, and they will keep a little better; but red orpiment and a little bone black, making as fine a pink as that properly ſo called, it will be beſt to uſe the latter.

R E D S.

Lake,
Vermilion, or
Cinnabar,
Minium, or
Red-lead,
Light-red, or
Light-oker calcined,
Brown-red, or
Brown-oker calcined
Indian-red,

are all properly qualified for encauſtic.

Cre

Care muft be taken to have the lake good ; that which is commonly fold under the name of Florence lacque, and recommended as the beft, is in general the worft; it is ufually in fmall hard grains, which hardnefs is owing to gum arabic, or what is worfe, to that glutinous fubftance which oozes out from the cherry tree, put in by the fabricant (of the lake) to bind and keep the grains together, and make it appear better merchandife than it really is; fuch lake will fcale off from the canvas; the gum it is impregnated with hinders the wax from penetrating its pores—every body knows that

lacque

lacque is made of cochineal; there is a baftard lake made of Brazil wood, but that is eafily known by its dulnefs. The beft lake for our purpofe is that which is of a fine, clear, deep hue, eafily to be broken and crumbled between the fingers. The fineft and beft lacque I ever faw and ufed, is made here in England by an ingenious artift in the feal engraving way.

Vermilion, or cinnabar, anfwers in encauftic all the purpofes it does in oil.

Minium, will be of infinite fervice for painting with the pencil

pencil and crayons; it will not change fixed with wax, as it does in oil; it may be ufed to advantage in fome carnations or flefh tints; and in landfcapes to enliven the oker, for great lights.

Light-red, or light-oker calcined, is of the fame univerfal ufe in this manner of painting as it is in oil, or common water colours.

Brown-red, or brown-oker calcined, may be employed for the fame ufe as in oil, or diftemper painting.

G 4   Indian-

Indian-red, the French call this colour, *Terre d'Angleterre*, Englifh earth; this colour is particularly ufeful for diftances, it makes the degradation of objects light and airy.

TERRA DI SIENA, and
TERRA VERTE,

Terra di Siena, a yellow hard and clayifh fubftance, fo called from the city of Siena in Italy, from whence it comes.

This colour is very unfit to be ufed crude, either for painting in encauftic or crayons, its pores are too clofe for the wax to penetrate; or to fay better,
this

this colour or earth is very much impregnated with a nitrous principle, with which wax cannot ſympathiſe, and for this very reaſon it is as unfit to be uſed crude in oil. Thoſe painters that uſe it freely have always but too much reaſon to repent. But,

Terra di Siena calcined, is a very beautiful and uſeful colour for all manner of painting, and particularly encauſtic. The fire having diſpelled in ſome meaſure the nitrous principle, the wax may freely enter its pores. This colour gives a great, ſoft, and glowing ſtrength in fleſh, drapery and landſcape;
ſome

ſome painters call this colour Roman oker.

Terra verte; this colour too comes to us from Italy, and ſome from Germany, they are both alike, and ought to be entirely baniſhed the pallette, as it grows ſo ſoon dirty and black when employed with oil. Terra verte differs from terra di Siena in little elſe but colour, it has a little vitriol. The too free uſe ſome of the older Italian painters made of this colour in fleſh tints, is the cauſe that numbers of pictures of thoſe maſters are ſo black as we ſee them at this time.

BLUES.

B L U E S.

Ultramarine,
Pruffian blue,
Smalt.

Ultramarine is perfectly good, and every body that likes to ufe it may do fo.

Pruffian blue, equals ultra-marine in encauftic, for all intents and purpofes; there is no other blue required for crayons neither.

Smalt may be ufed, but I think it rather too gritty; its particles are too tranfparent for

parts

parts where a ſolid maſs of colour is required. For crayons
it does very well mixed with
Pruſſian blue to bind it, both
together make a beautiful colour, the grittineſs of ſmalt
will there be of advantage.
This colour will not grow black
fixed with wax as it does in
oil.

B L A C K S.

Ivory Black,
Bone Black
Blue Black,
have all the neceſſary qualifications to be employed.

Ivory black may be em-
ployed for all the uſes made of
it in oil.

Blue

Blue black is particularly neceſſary for landſcapes; the blue black generally ſold at the colour ſhops is commonly made of wine ſtalks; but blue black made of peach, apricot, or plum-ſtones calcined, is by far the beſt; it is not ſo looſe and ſpungy as the former, its colour too is finer.

Bone black is the moſt valuable of the black tribe for ſweetneſs, and a tranſparent warmth for landſcapes and figures; bone black and white alone will make ſofter and more natural turning tints than any other colours can produce; the

the Flemiſh painters uſe it very much for glazing.

This black mixed with a little terra di Siena calcined, makes the ſtrongeſt and ſweeteſt ſhades that can be obtained with colours.

The beſt is made of the bones of mutton trotters calcined.

COLLEN's EARTH.

A dark blackiſh brown and ſomewhat bituminous earth, inclining a little towards purple, is a very good colour, and of ſingular uſe where extraordinary

dinary ſtrength is required in fore grounds.

U M B R A,
Crude and calcined.

A uſeful colour enough for common purpoſes ; ſome painters uſe it for ſhades in fleſh, but very improperly, for it is a very raw colour crude or calcined, and only fit to be uſed in drapery or back grounds.

Theſe are all the colours that ought to be uſed for painting in encauſtic, with the pencil ; there are a few more that might be employed in this manner, but as they are rather

ther inferior in quality, or only compounds of thofe already mentioned, I omit them; a few, not commonly ufed in oil painting that notwithftanding might be ufed in encauftic, I fhall mention under the article of crayons, as they belong more to, and are more ufeful in that way.

E N-

ENCAUSTIC;

O R,

Method of painting with and fixing of the CRAYONS.

THE method of painting with and fixing of the crayons comes not only within the fenfe of encauftic, but is the very felf-fame thing. The whole proceeding is founded upon the foregoing principle; the fame materials and agent are required.—The only dif-ference between painting in en-cauftic with the pencil, and painting in encauftic with cray-

H   ons,

ons, confifts in employing the colours; in the former—you paint with colours tempered with water; in the latter—you employ, and paint with the fame colours dry; the effect and folidity will be equal and the fame in both.——

The encomiums I beftowed upon the penciling fyftem, are applicable to that of the crayons; I fhall fay nothing more; experience will be the beft panegyrift. I am afraid crayons, as feemingly the lefs troublefome, will carry the golden apple; I will not anticipate the decifion of the public.—I fhall give the hint, and my fellow artifts

artifts may make ufe of it as
they pleafe.——

As the fyftem of encauftic
for the pencil is the parent of
that for the · crayons, and as
both · may be happily blended
and jointly practifed to good
purpofe, I fhall, to avoid tire-
fomely repeating the fame thing
over again, refer the reader to
the former procefs whenever
fimilarities of proceeding occur ; they, befides comment-
ing each other, will open to
the more timorous artift a freer
field of action. As I did in
the former, fo fhall I in this,
give that method of proceed-

ing,

ing, which by experience I found to be the best.

Though this system did not enter in the original plan of publication with the other, and I intended to withold it from the public a little longer, to see what reception the former should meet with; yet as it got vent by shewing it to few friends, and a gentleman offering me (in his opinion) a considerable reward to dispose of the secret in his favour only, I, to prevent some modern PLINY's casting more direct reflexions upon me, without my having the skill of Apelles to uphold my reputation,

at

at leaſt thought proper to give them to the public both at once. To make diſcoveries that may be of infinite advantage to arts, ſubſervient to private avarice, is the foible of a weak, jealous, and ill-natured mind. —Here follows the proceſs; and firſt the preparation of the cloth.

H 3   A R T.

A R T. I.

Preparation of the cloth, or paper, for painting with crayons.

FIRST method to prepare the cloth without paper.

Take any ſort of linen cloth whoſe texture is pretty cloſe and even, ſtretch it upon a ſtraining frame and rub it on the back with a piece of wax, as directed under Art. the firſt, page 26. your cloth waxed, prepare any tint or colour you like, or judge beſt for a ground to work upon, let enter into the compoſition of this tint or colour, one half, or at leaſt one

one third of chalk or whitening, mix and temper all with
pure water ; your tint ready,
paint-over your cloth with it
on that ſide you are to paint
upon, and lay the colour on
pretty even and ſubſtantially;
this colour or ground dry,
bring the canvas near the fire,
as under Art. the fourth, page
35. and the wax melting will
fix that colour or ground,
which when cool will be a fit
and firm body to work up-
on with crayons. Note, if the
quantity of wax ſhould prove
too ſmall for the quantity of
colour, apply with a bruſh on
the back ſome wax diſſolved
in turpentine, as deſcribed in

H 4   the

the next page, and bring the canvas again to the fire. It is effential in painting with cray-ons to have the firft ground properly prepared.

Second method, to prepare cloth with paper pafted thereon.

TAKE linen cloth and ftretch it upon a frame as the foregoing ; then make a pafte with fine wheat flour, or ftarch and water, and when the pafte is near boiled enough, put in and mix with it of com-mon horfe-turpentine, about half an ounce to fix ounces of pafte, ftir it well together, and let it fimmer five or fix mi-

nutes

nutes longer; then take it from the fire and set it by to cool a little, and while it is still tolerably warm, paste your paper (grey, blue or white) to the cloth in the usual manner, and set it by to dry.—In the mean time put wax, broken in small pieces, to dissolve in oil of turpentine near a fire, and in such proportion that, when dissolved and cold, it will be of consistence like a thin paste, and fluent enough to be managed with a brush.—When your cloth and paper is perfectly dry, hold it over or before a fire, at a convenient distance, and with a brush apply the dissolved wax on both
sides

ſides to cloth and paper, and continue laying on wax till you perceive both ſurfaces equally ſhining, and there be no imbibed-like ſpot remaining; this done, let your cloth ſtand before the fire about half an hour longer, (or in ſummer in the ſun,) and, the oil of turpentine evaporating, the wax will become firm again, and be fit to receive any tint or colour for a ground to work upon, which you muſt lay on and fix as the foregoing upon cloth without paper, and when cool you may go to work.

A R T.

A R T. II.

*Of the crayons their prepa-
ration and use.*

PREPARATION. There is no
particular or uncommon
preparation or compofition required for encauftic, all crayons hitherto commonly ufed
may be employed; fome great
lights only will be wanted for
every fet of tints; for what has
been faid on colours, and their
growing deeper when fixed
with wax, *penciling fyftem Art.*
II. *page* 29, 30. holds equally
here; therefore every artift,
that may be inclined to make
a trial in this manner, will do
well

well to make an effay of all his tints, by preparing a piece of cloth as directed in the fore-going article, and giving a few ftrokes of each crayon and fix-ing it, this will immediately fhew what new tints will be wanted.

In compofing any new tint it will be well to leave out ful-lers-earth, pipe-clay, chalk, and other calcarious matters * which are generally ufed in the common way ; the former—to bind the loofer

* Fullers-earth, pipe-clay, chalk, &c. ought to be left out, becaufe they fink fo very low when fixed with wax, and impart a great dullnefs to all thofe tints wherein they prevail ; pipe-clay and fullers-earth a dufky tranfparent gray; chalk, a yellowifh-white no-colour.

looſer colours; the latter—to keep up the flake-white and white-lead, which otherwiſe would turn black ; in encauſtic thoſe matters are wanted for none of the above ends; flake-white and white-lead will not change, and both together will make a body ſufficiently connected to bind the lighter tints.

All colours uſed in oil and mentioned in the foregoing liſt, are good for crayons, and no others.

Note. What has been ſaid at the end of the liſt of colours, that a few more colours, not commonly employed in oil, might

might be uſed for crayons, was a miſtake of the author's upon his experimental table; there are but two more that may be uſed for crayons, viz. bice and verditer.

The uſe of the crayons in en-cauſtic is the very ſame as commonly practiſed, there is no difference; you muſt work and paint upon the waxed ground as you do upon the bare paper. Encauſtic has the advantage over the common way as to expedition. The fine grittineſs procured by the particles of the chalk mixed with the ground you work upon, will *file* off more colour from the

crayon

crayon than the grain of the unwaxed paper ; and the wax diffuſed through the ground will retain the colours better ; ſo that when you ſweeten your tints with your finger there will be no waſte ; for in working, the particles of the colour will intrude themſelves into the body of the wax, which yields to them ; which paper, bare or prepared with a ground tempered with gum or ſize, does not.

A R T.

A R T. III.

How to fix the crayons.

FOR fixing the crayons you muſt act and proceed in every reſpect, according to the directions given *penciling ſyſtem Art.* VI. *page* 35, 36, &c. you may retouch, and apply the diſſolved wax on the back, and bring the picture to the fire as often as required.

Obſer-

*Obſervations on the ſyſtem for
painting with crayons.*

FOR painting with crayons
I ſhould prefer cloth prepared according to the firſt
method, without paper, for the
ſame reaſon I gave for deviating
from Count Caylus's ſyſtem,
page 48, 49. however, artiſts
may decide for themſelves.

Beſides the two methods
mentioned for preparing the
cloth, one might paint upon
paper paſted upon cloth as directed, without firſt laying on
any wax or preparatory ground ;
but ſuch paintings would not
have that laſting ſolidity they
I   ought;

ought; beſides, laying on a ground preparatory and analogous in hue to the ſubject to be painted, is more expeditious, as ſuch a ground may be made to ſerve for a half tint, and anſwers the purpoſe of dead colouring.

Turpentine enters in the paſte for one great and principal end, viz. to keep the particles of the paſte a little aſunder, and facilitate to the wax a free paſſage through it; for the particles of turpentine diffuſed through the paſte, in melting, when the picture is brought near the fire, open ſo many equi-diſtant channels for the wax, which, by this means, can

can penetrate freely and uniformly, and diffufe itfelf over
the whole in equal proportion;
without the turpentine it would
not fucceed fo well; the wax
would only come through here
and there; the colours would
in a manner be calcined before
a fufficient quantity could penetrate to fecure them; for
though there will be wax e-
nough for the firft fixing, yet,
to alter or retouch, or where an
extraordinary great body of colours might be employed, there
might be a deficiency of wax,
which cannot be fupplied other-
wife than by laying it on, on
the back, and if it could not

I 2   work

work its its paſſage through the whole might miſcarry. *

As few artiſts compoſe the crayons themſelves, and as inſerting directions for that purpoſe would have ſwelled this treatiſe too much ; the author, for the conveniency of all practitioners has given the *recipe* of proportion for compoſing every tint for what it is to be when fixed, to Mr. Sandys, colour merchant, in Dirty-lane Long-acre, of whom perfect ſets may be

* Old crayon pictures may be fixed very well ; the paſte becoming old looſes its coheſion ; the wax may freely and uniformly penetrate through ; they will want retouching. If any artiſt has a mind to try, he may do it with ſome inſignificant ſubject for fear of miſcarrying on a firſt tryal.

be had ; and as the author has communicated the *recipe*, for binding the moſt difficult colours, * for the benefit of the art, without fee or reward whatſoever, thoſe crayons will be ſold at the uſual price. At the above place, may be had cloth or paper ready prepared on ſhort notice.

However, if any artiſt ſhould chuſe to prepare the crayons himſelf, he will do well to leave out the pipe-clay, fullers-earth, chalk, &c. as much as poſſible, and mix his tints as

I 3   uſual.

* If this treatiſe ſhould meet with ſuch approbation as to require a ſecond edition, the recipe for the compoſing of crayons will be inſerted at full length.

ufual. The ftandard recommended under *Art.* II. *page* 29, 30. and explained *page* 55, 56. will be of fervice for afcertaining beforehand the value of each tint.

If any crayon prepared for the old way, fhould prove too hard for this, as may be the cafe with vermilion, bice, verditer, and the other loofer colours, in whofe compofition enters a little pafte to bind them, fprinkle thofe crayons with a brufh dipt in fpirit of wine, and they will become manageable.

G E N E-

GENERAL REMARKS

On the apparent characters of
encauſtic paintings, on wax
and varniſh.

THE principal apparent
characters of an encauſtic
painting are,

1. The colours have all the
airineſs of water colours, and
all the ſtrength of paintings in
oil, without partaking of the
apparent character, or defects
of either.

2. You may look at and en-
joy a picture in any light; the
colours are bright, freſh and
lively

lively without glaring. They require no varniſh.

3. The colours are firm, without being brittle, and will bear ſcratching without receiving any harm.

The effect of the colours is the ſame in both ſyſtems, each will have and preſerve its peculiar character, as to the manner of painting; if you paint your ſubject in the light and airy ſtile of the Carlo Marat ſchool, when the colours will be fixed you will have the high colouring of Rubens.

On

On WAX.

It is not material for me to decide which of the two ought to be preferably employed, bees-wax ſimple, or virgin-wax.—— For large works that will be expoſed to the air, I ſhould prefer the former; artiſts will ſee by a few trials which will ſuit their taſte beſt.

On VARNISH.

Varniſhes are not required, as has already been obſerved; but as our eyes have been uſed ſo much to ſee colours, not in their natural hue, but diſguiſed by varniſh, thoſe

that

that fhould like to pleafe them-
felves in this point may ufe the
following method.

First lay on with a clean
fpunge a fubftantial lay of the
white of eggs, and work it well
upon the picture. This dry,
lay on any varnifh commonly
ufed for oil-painting, and your
picture will look as if painted
with oil-colours.

This varnifh may be taken
off at pleafure, the uppermoft
by rubbing the furface of the
picture with a rag dipped in
fpirit of wine or turpentine,
the white of eggs by wafhing
the picture with water. It is
not

not adviſeable to lay a varniſh of ſpirits or gums, without firſt uſing the white of eggs, as ſpirit of turpentine is the menſtruum of wax.

EXPERIMENTS.

TO adopt and practife in earneft any new fyftem without fufficient trials and proofs of its merit, may be called going wilfully aftray.—— To avoid deceiving myfelf in the new fyftem before us, I, after having been convinced of its advantageous practicability, fet about to afcertain the other great point, the ftability of the colours; for this end, and to know more exactly how much every colour would vary from its original hue in a certain fpace of time, as well in regard to the fame fyftem as in

oppo-

oppofition to oil-colours, I pro-
ceeded as follows.

Experiment the firſt and prin-cipal, 1757.

I had all the colours ufed
in oil painting, mentioned in
the foregoing lift, carefully
ground with water, at Mr.
Sandys's, colour-merchant, and
from thofe colours I compofed
ninety various and fenfibly differing tints, for flefh, drapery
and landfcape ; of each tint
I had a quantity of a two
ounce gallipot full, tempered
with water; fo I left them well
fcreened from duft till they
were become dry again ; then I
divided

divided each mafs of tint in four equal parts; two of each I fet by for the comparative ufe, the other two parts of each I employed in the following manner.

One part of each I tempered again with water, and painted with it over a fpace of cloth of fix inches wide and two inches high, the tints clofe to each other, in the manner of cop-per-plate, *page* 58. and the cloth waxed as directed *Art*. IV. *page* 26. The fame I did with the entire and unmixed colours.

The

The other parts of each tint I tempered with the fineft nut-oil according to cuftom, and painted-over with them fuch another fpace of fix inches by two, as the former, upon oil-cloth. The fame I did with the entire colours, and fet them by to dry; when dry, I brought the encauftic tints near the fire, and by melting the wax fixed them.

My tints thus ready, I cut each piece of cloth, encauftic and oil-tints, in five equal parts, and difpofed of a piece of each in the following manner.

1. One

1. One piece of each I expoſed in the open air to all the
injuries of ſun, dew, wind and
rain.

2. One piece of each I nail-
ed to a wall in a damp cellar-
like room.

3. One piece of each I nail-
ed- to the cieling of a kitchen
and near the chimney, where all
the year round a fire was kept.

4. One piece of each I nail-
ed to the ſide of a room I uſu-
ally inhabited.

5. One piece of each I put
between ſeveral quires of paper,
and

and confined them in a cloſe drawer deprived of air.

Thus I left them, till the latter end of October. 1759, (the ſpace of twenty-ſeven months) when I gathered them. Then I took the two parts of tints I had ſet by and preſerved, and tempering the one with water, and the other with oil, painted the firſt upon a freſh piece of waxed cloth and fixed them, the other tempered with oil, I painted upon a freſh piece of oil-cloth, and after having waſhed the old tints, on comparing the new and old colours together found as follows.

K   The

The old encauſtic entire colours and tints of number 1.
ſeemed to have ſuffered a con-
ſiderable change in oppoſition
to the new ones, but compared
to their old fellows in oil they
looked bright.

I waſhed them both with
common water, and a bruſh,
the encauſtic tints recovered
a little; oil-tints not.

I brought the encauſtic to
the fire, and moſt tints recovered their original hue, and
were equal to the new ones,
*pinks, yellow-orpiment, lake, ter-
ra di Siena,* and *verditer* excepted,

cepted; the firſt was partly gone, what remained was dull; the ſecond was grown whiter; *lake* grown lighter, but had not ſuffered in beauty of colour; *terra di Siena* crude, grown rough and dirty; *verditer*, a little dull.

No. 3. ſeemed to have ſuffered by the ſmoke; but after waſhing it with a ſtout bruſh, and ſoap and water, it recovered its original hue, *pinks*, *yellow-orpiment*, *ſmalt* and *verditer* excepted; the firſt was ſenſibly decayed; the ſecond grown darker, inclining towards red-orpiment; the third grown dull, but mixed with Pruſſian-blue

it

it was as bright as the new; verditer grown dark and dull.

No. 2, 4, 5. were juſt as the new ones, there was no difference.

Oil colours did not ſtand the teſt ſo well ; their general appearance in oppoſition to old and new encauſtic,—was :

No 1. weak, dull and dim, ſome entirely gone.

No. 2. freckled, of all ſorts of hues, not to be waſhed off.

No. 3. darker, ſome dull, others dirty, ſome entirely gone.

No. 4.

No. 4. conſiderably yellower, and leſs bright.

No. 5. yellow-ſpotted, as if varniſhed with gall.

The foregoing tints were all fixed with virgin wax, which I thought the beſt; but having at the ſame time and with the ſame colours painted upon cloth waxed with common yellow bees-wax, I found that the latter in the open air preſerved the colours rather better.

K 3   *Expe-*

Experiment the ſecond.

I waſhed the foregoing tints with *a ſtrong lixivium of pot-aſh, vinegar, ſpirit of wine, a ſolution of ſea ſalt, and aqua fortis.*

By this operation the oil-colours were entirely deſtroyed, the encauſtic ſuffered nothing, only *ſmalt* grew darker ; but after ſcraping it and bringing it again to the fire, it recovered its tone.

I have ſtill a little ſcrap of a picture, a landſcape, by me, which has undergone all the above-

abovementioned trials and more, for I took it from the frame and folded it in four, put it upon the frame again, and brought to the fire and the folds diſappeared,—the colours are as freſh as if painted but yeſterday. On examining it cloſe one may perceive it ſuffered violence, but at a yard's diſtance no marks appear.

Experiment on oil-colours.

Having perceived that oil-colours, painted upon a waxed ground always appeared brighter upon an oil-cloth; I, to come at the knowledge of the cauſe of this effect, contrived

K 4 various

various experiments, but without ſucceſs; at laſt I made microſcopical obſervations, and found that oil-colours painted upon an oil-cloth undergo a great fermentation, five or ſix hours after being laid on, and continue ſo till they are dry. Then they begin to overcaſt, and by degrees cover the ſurface with a yellowiſh, grey ſubſtance, not to be waſhed or rubbed off but with a knife.

Among the very ſame colours painted upon an encauſtic ground I could perceive no ſuch fermentation, or overcaſting.—From this we may conjecture that the priming, or
ground

ground we work upon is more
the caufe of the colours changing than the colours them-
felves, very likely owing to
the defecated faline particles of
the oil, which are diffolved by
and mix with the new oil and
colours ; or to the fuperabun-
dant quantity of falts contain-
ed in the ground or priming,
which is generally compofed
of the coarfeft oil and colours,
and frequently half chalk.

Though this latter experiment
has nothing to do with encauftic,
it will find its application and
owner.

To

To prove the ſtability of encauſtic colours, I have mentioned but two experiments; they are ſufficient; from them we may draw the following

CONCLUSIONS.

Firſt, that encauſtic colours, having refiſted the injuries of the weather better than oil-colours, for the ſpace of twenty-ſeven months, they will prove more laſting than oil-colours for a greater ſpace of time.

Secondly, that having refiſted the effects of the corroſives, *alkali* and *aqua fortis*, &c. the circumambient air, howſoever impregnated with saline

ſaline particles, cannot affect them.

Thirdly, that if pictures of this kind receive any hurt, fire will reſtore them.

The moſt celebrated men of antiquity, celebrated the per-formances of their painters ; if their colours had not been as laſting as their ſkill was great, ſome one might have left us regretful inſtances. They left us none.

Was WAX the preſerver of their colours ?

F I N I S.

Advertisement.

AS the foregoing Treatise is written and publifhed with an intention to communicate a difcovery that will prove of infinite advantage to the lovelieft of arts, in all its branches; the author, confcious of wanting the neceffary qualifications of a writer in a language not natural to him, hopes for indulgence, for all the inaccuracies and improprieties of expreffion he may and muft have fallen into : as to facts, he begs leave to affure the public, that nothing has been advanced but what is ftrictly true.

If any artift or others fhould in practifing be at a lofs or ftand for any thing, the author fhall always be willing and ready to give them farther light on any occafion.

The treatife on Practical Painting in general, which was to have been publifhed together with this, as has been intimated to the public in an advertifement of the third of January, will be publifhed as foon as poffible ; the author being engaged in a work of a very extenfive nature, had not time to bring it in perfect order himfelf ; a gentleman and friend of his has been fo kind as to undertake the finifhing and correcting of it ; it will foon be ready for the prefs.

TABLE of CONTENTS.

TABLE of CONTENTS.

1   Art.

TABLE of CONTENTS.